D0471371

. . . for parents and teachers

Death, divorce, physical separation, and other forms of loss are all emotionally difficult experiences. They require all of our personal resources in working through our feelings.

For a young child, coping with the loss of a friend who is moving away can be just as difficult as coping with a more severe loss. It is crucial that children going through any such loss be able to express their attitudes and feelings.

My Best Friend Moved Away touches upon many of the emotions accompanying such an event. It provides an especially suitable background for the discussion of the feelings involved in any type of loss.

I encourage parents, teachers, and other professionals to facilitate the sharing of emotions through the sharing of this story.

MANUEL S. SILVERMAN, Ph.D.
ASSOCIATE PROFESSOR AND CHAIR
DEPARTMENT OF GUIDANCE
AND COUNSELING
LOYOLA UNIVERSITY OF CHICAGO

Copyright © 1980, Raintree Publishers Inc.

All rights reserved. No part of this book may be
reproduced or utilized in any form or by any means,
electronic or mechanical, including photocopying,
recording, or by any information storage and retrieval
system, without permission in writing from the Publisher.
Inquiries should be addressed to Raintree Childrens Books,
205 West Highland Avenue, Milwaukee, Wisconsin 53203.

Library of Congress Number: 79-24111

2 3 4 5 6 7 8 9 0 84 83 82 81

Printed in the United States of America.

Library of Congress Cataloging in Publication Data

Zelonky, Joy.
   My best friend moved away.

   SUMMARY: When his best friend moves away, Brian
tries to cope with his feelings of loss and separation.
   [1.   Friendship — Fiction.   2.   Moving, Household
— Fiction]   I.   Adams, Angela.   II.   Title.
PZ7.Z398My   [Fic]   79-24111
ISBN 0-8172-1353-8 lib. bdg.

MY BEST FRIEND MOVED AWAY

by Joy Zelonky

illustrated by Angela Adams

introduction by Manuel S. Silverman, Ph.D.

RAINTREE CHILDRENS BOOKS
Milwaukee • Toronto • Melbourne • London

I was starting to get worried about
Nick. I waited and waited at the corner
where we were supposed to meet, but there
was no sign of him. If we were late again,
I just knew Mrs. Hernandez was going to
make us stay after school.

I especially didn't want Nick to be late
for school. Some of the kids tease him
about being slow because he has to wear a
leg brace. I think Nick gets around better
than just about anyone else I know.

Finally I saw him coming toward me.
He looked ready to burst with excitement.

"Guess what!" Nick shouted. "My mom and dad bought a new house!"

I just stared at him for a minute. Then I asked, "Why did they do that?"

He came up to me, and we started walking toward school.

"Because our house isn't big enough," he said.

"I like your house. It looks a lot like ours."

"I like it too," Nick said. "It's just too small. My mom's having a baby soon. We need more room."

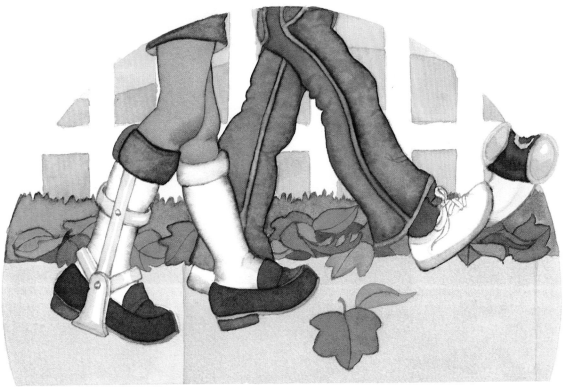

I wasn't sure I liked Nick's news, but I didn't want to tell him that. "Does that mean we can't walk to school together anymore?" I asked.

"Oh, I won't even be going to this school. Our new house is across town. I'm going to another school in a few weeks."

Now I was positive that I didn't like Nick's news. I couldn't stop thinking about it all day. Nick was my best friend. How could he move away? It didn't seem fair.

After school, Nick and I walked home together, as usual.

"Do you want to shoot some marbles?" I asked.

"I can't," he said. "Some people are coming over to look at our house tonight. I have to clean my room before they come."

After Nick had gone inside his house, I
looked at the For Sale sign in the front
yard. Then I had an idea. I thought that if
Nick's parents couldn't sell their house,
then maybe they wouldn't move away!

Carefully I looked up and down the
block. The only person on the whole street
was the girl who delivers the papers.

After the girl had gone on to the next
street, I crept over to the sign. I ripped
the sign off its post and threw it as far as I
could. Then I ran all the way home.

The next morning, Nick met me on the corner.

"Did you sell your house?" I asked, trying to act like I hoped the answer was yes.

"Maybe," Nick said. "The people liked it. But they almost didn't show up."

I felt my face turning red. "What do you mean?"

"Someone took our For Sale sign and threw it in the street. What a dirty trick! My dad finally found it and put it back up just in time."

Each day after that, more people looked at Nick's house. I didn't try to tear the sign down again. I knew it was wrong to have done that. Also, it was nailed down too tightly.

One morning Nick was already at the corner when I got there.

"We sold our house!" he called.

"That's nice." Nick looked so happy that I just couldn't tell him how miserable I felt. "When are you moving?" I asked.

"Not for a month. That gives us plenty of time to play!"

After that, Nick and I did something together almost every day. Sometimes we played games with other kids, but usually it was just Nick and me.

We traded all of our comic books back and forth. We flew kites and sailed boats in the park. When it rained, we stayed inside and built forts out of blankets. We played a million games of marbles.

Then came moving day.

I went over to Nick's to say good-bye.

Nick waved from the car and said, "I wish you were moving too."

I took a small bag out of my pocket and handed it to him. "I . . . I want you to have these for a going-away present."

Nick's eyes grew wide. "Marbles," he whispered. "But these are your best ones."

"You're my best friend," I answered.

"Thanks, Brian. When you come over, you can use them, okay?"

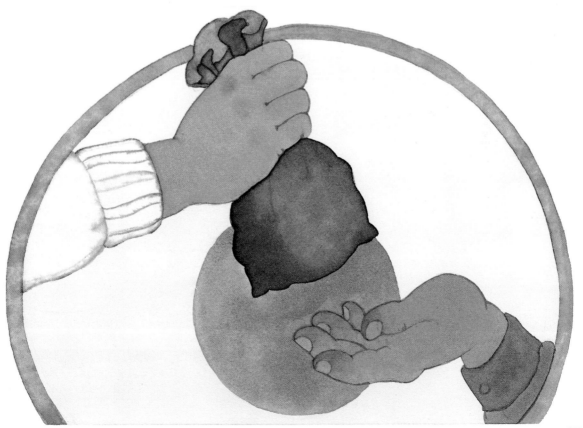

I nodded, waved good-bye, and went home. I sat on my bed and looked at the ceiling for a long time. I had never felt so bad. It was worse than the time my bicycle was stolen. At least that hadn't made me *lonely*.

Finally my dad came in and sat on the bed with me. "It's hard to be the one left behind, isn't it?" he said. "I'm sure you'll make new friends."

Dad didn't understand at all. "I'll never have a friend like Nick," I told him.
"You're right," he said. "No two people are alike. That's why each friend is special."

Dad was right about Nick being special. I just about died of loneliness during the next few weeks. Then Nick called me and invited me to his new house.

My dad and I took the subway across town. He went on to do some shopping while I visited Nick.

"Come on!" said Nick. "I want to show you my room."

Nick's room was large and very nice. I was a little jealous.

After showing me around, Nick asked, "What do you want to do now?"

"How about flying a kite?"

"That's for babies," said Nick. "None of the kids around here do that."

"Then let's shoot marbles."

Nick shook his head. "That's dumb too. I'll tell you what — if you promise to keep it a secret, I'll take you somewhere really great."

I said okay, and Nick led me outside. We walked around the corner to an area where a new house was being built.

I looked around. "This looks kind of dangerous," I said.

"You sound just like my mom," Nick scoffed. "All the kids come here. It's fun — watch!"

Nick walked all the way across a board that stretched over a big hole. "Follow the leader," he called back to me.

I looked down. Muddy water filled the bottom of the hole.

"Chicken!" yelled Nick.

I took a deep breath and started across. Every time I took a step, the board wiggled. I tried to keep my balance by leaning from side to side. I wondered how Nick could possibly have done this with his leg brace. He must have practiced a lot. . . .

Splash! Down I fell.

"Are you all right?" asked Nick.

"I think so," I said shakily. I was too scared and wet to say much else.

"We'd better go back," Nick said. "You're no good at this."

Nick's mother took one look at us and knew where we'd been. She helped me clean up.

"Nick, I warned you not to play there," she said. "Brian could have been hurt, and you too. Maybe you'll learn to listen to me if you stay home all day tomorrow."

"Oh, Mom," Nick said. Then he turned to me. "It's all your fault. Now I can't do things with my friends tomorrow!"

I stared at Nick for a minute. Then I ran outside and met my dad on the sidewalk.

"What happened?" he asked. "Did you and Nick have a fight?"

"No, but Nick is so different now. He's not like the old Nick at all." The rest of the way to the subway, I explained what had happened.

"I bet Nick's not as happy as you think he is," said my dad. "This must be a hard time for him too. He has to make friends in a strange place. He has to get used to a new school. Everything's changed for him. Nick's changed too."

I tried looking at things from Nick's point of view and had to admit my dad was right.

"But why did he have to change?" I asked. "I liked Nick the way he was."

"The people you know won't always stay the same," he answered. "Sometimes all you can do is remember the good times you've shared."

I looked at my reflection in the subway
window. "Will I change too?"

"What do you think?"

"I guess I will. But if I'm careful,
maybe the good things about me will get
better."

Suddenly I stood up. "Hey, Dad, could we get off now?"

"But it's not our stop yet."

"I know," I said. "But there's a good store that has marbles right here. I promised some kids down the block that I'd play marbles, and I gave all of my good ones to Nick, and —"

"Let's go!" said my dad.